"Hi!" I hollered. "Who are you?"

The boy was little. Not that little, but littler than I am. He had curly hair and a striped T-shirt and dark brown skin.

A little voice came out of him: "Nobody."

Then, without another word, he walked away.

"What's the big idea?" I said.

The boy ran off into the woods.

That boy had made me mad. Who needs a Nobody Boy anyway?

Other books by Sharon Dennis Wyeth:

Ginger Brown: Too Many Houses
Always My Dad
Vampire Bugs: Stories Conjured from the Past
The World of Daughter McGuire

GINGER BROWN:
The Nobody Boy

by Sharon Dennis Wyeth

**illustrated by Cornelius Van Wright
and Ying-Hwa Hu**

A FIRST STEPPING STONE BOOK

Random House New York

For Sheri and Kristie Dennis

Text copyright © 1997 by Sharon Dennis Wyeth
Illustrations copyright © 1997,by Cornelius Van Wright and Ying-Hwa Hu.
All rights reserved under International and Pan-American Copyright Conventions.
Published in the United States by Random House, Inc., New York, and simultaneously
in Canada by Random House of Canada Limited, Toronto.

http://www.randomhouse.com/

Library of Congress Cataloging-in-Publication Data
Wyeth, Sharon Dennis.
Ginger Brown: the Nobody Boy/by Sharon Dennis Wyeth.
    p. cm.
"A First stepping stone book."
SUMMARY: Ginger's summer at her grandparents' home in the country is
enlivened by the appearance of a sad little boy who calls himself Nobody.
ISBN 0-679-85645-5 (trade) — ISBN 0-679-95645-X (lib. bdg.)
[1. Country life—Fiction. 2. Friendship—Fiction.] I. Title.
PZ7.W9746Gg 1997
[Fic]—dc20   96-38207

Printed in the United States of America
10 9 8 7 6 5 4 3 2 1
Random House, Inc.   New York, Toronto, London, Sydney, Auckland

Contents

1

Visiting

This summer, I was down-the-country on my grandparents' farm. I was far away from my parents, just like last summer. Only this summer I wasn't six. I was seven.

I was outside Mama and Papa Brown's barn. I was drawing a picture. A picture of my family.

First I drew Mommy. I colored her face brown and her dress blue.

I drew Daddy and colored him white

and gave him a yellow trumpet.

Then I drew me—Ginger Brown.

I gave myself tan skin and lots of squiggly hair, which I have. I made myself tall, which I am.

Finally, I drew my cat, Leo, who is orange.

Then I stopped drawing and looked up. Leo was sitting on somebody's lap! A somebody I'd never seen before—a boy. He was in our yard, sitting in my swing, holding my cat!

"Hi!" I hollered. "Who are you?"

The boy didn't say anything. He just looked down at the ground. He was little. Not that little, but littler than I am. He had curly hair and a striped T-shirt and dark brown skin.

"Hi," I said, walking over. "Who are

you? Where did you come from?"

The boy looked up at me, but he still didn't say anything.

"That's my cat," I said, pointing to Leo. "His name is Leo. What's your name?"

The boy still didn't say anything. He patted Leo on the head.

"You're quiet," I said. "What's wrong? Cat got your tongue?"

Papa Brown says that to me when I'm quiet. I thought it was a good joke, so I laughed.

But the boy didn't.

I took Leo off his lap.

"You're sitting on my swing," I said.

The boy frowned and stood up.

"But that's okay—"

He sat down.

"Who are you?" I asked him again.

A little voice came out of the boy: "Nobody."

"Nobody?" I stared into his face. "Well, my name is Ginger," I said. "We are the only two kids around here."

I put Leo down on the ground.

"Want a push?" I asked.

"Okay," said the boy in a little voice.

I walked behind the swing. I pushed him a bit and he swung his legs. I looked at his face, but he wasn't smiling. I guessed that he was shy.

Too bad he is so little, I thought. But even playing with a little kid would be better than playing all by myself.

"Where do you live?" I asked.

The boy sighed. "Nowhere."

I stopped pushing the swing. He got

up and I stood right in front of him.

"You have to live somewhere," I said. "Where are your parents?"

Suddenly, the boy got quiet again. It looked as if he might cry!

"Sorry," I said. "I didn't mean to make you sad."

"That's okay," said the boy.

Without another word, he walked away.

"What's the big idea?" I said.

The boy kept walking.

This boy is strange, I thought, *and not too polite. First he pets my cat and sits on my swing without even asking. Now he won't even play!*

"Where are you going?" I hollered.

"Home," he said, turning around.

"See? You *do* live somewhere," I said,

skipping behind him. "Why don't you stay? I know a lot of games we could play."

The boy began to run. He ran across the field. He ran right into the woods.

"You could say good-bye!" I yelled after him.

He disappeared into the trees without a wave.

"Leave then!" I shouted when I couldn't see him anymore. "Who needs a Nobody Boy, anyway?"

Papa Brown came out of the barn.

"Who are you talking to?"

I stuck out my lip. That boy had made me mad. "Nobody."

"Talking to yourself, eh?" Papa Brown chuckled.

"No," I said, "I'm talking to Nobody."

I pointed to the woods. "He lives back there."

Papa Brown stuck his hands under the straps of his overalls. "Nobody lives back there but an old hermit named Evans."

"A hermit!" I said. I had heard about hermit crabs in school. They hide inside their hard shells. I wondered what a hermit person looked like.

"Are you sure nobody else lives in the woods?" I asked.

"The woods are thorny," said Papa Brown. "Don't reckon anybody else would want to live in there."

But I knew someone else did live in there. Nobody did.

Into the Woods

The next day when I woke up, my covers were on the floor. I had had a bad dream! I dreamed that I had run into the hermit in the woods. He was tall and skinny and had a horrible laugh. And where his ears were supposed to be, there were giant crabs!

I ran downstairs to the kitchen. "Morning, pumpkin," said Mama Brown. I hugged Mama Brown's waist. She had on her sunflower apron. Her feet were bare because she doesn't like shoes.

I poured myself a big glass of juice and Mama Brown gave me some pancakes.

Papa Brown came in from outdoors.

"What are your plans for the day?" he asked me.

I tried to talk, but my mouth was too full. "Dime going to find doughbody."

"What?" said Papa Brown.

"I think she said she's going exploring," said Mama Brown. She patted me on the hair.

I jumped up and put on my baseball cap. I had to find the Nobody Boy before it was too late.

Mama Brown gave me a bucket. "If you see any of those fat blackberries," she said, "pick me some and we'll bake a pie."

"Okay," I said, hurrying out with Leo. The back door banged shut. I ran with the bucket, not stopping to pick any berries. I had to warn the Nobody Boy about the hermit.

I ran into the trees and followed the path. I had been in the woods with my father and grandparents, but never by myself. I hoped that I wouldn't run into the hermit.

I looked down at Leo. Leo had sharp claws. Maybe he would protect me. But just at that moment, I scratched myself on a thornbush.

"Ouch!" I cried. I started to run. "Hello!" I called out. "Are you back here, Nobody?"

"Hello!" a small voice answered.

I hopped off the path and ran toward the voice. I stopped in front of a creek. I'd been there once before with Papa Brown.

Sitting on a rock with his feet in the water was Nobody.

"Thank goodness I found you," I said, sitting down next to him. "I came to warn you about the hermit!"

"What's that?" he said.

"A person who has ears that look like crabs!"

The Nobody Boy looked scared.

"He's a monster who lives in these woods, all by himself! He calls himself Mr. Evans! But he's an ugly old hermit!"

The boy stuck his chin in my face. "He is not!" he said. His voice was very loud. "He's my grandfather!"

"Your grandfather?"

"Yes," he said. "Mr. Evans is not a hermit, he's my granddad."

"Oh," I said, feeling kind of confused. "Sorry."

The Nobody Boy picked up a rock and tossed it into the creek. The rock went *plink, plink, plink* and made three big circles.

"That's neat," I said. I picked up a rock and tried it, but my rock just sank.

Nobody picked up another rock and made three more circles.

"How do you do that?" I asked.

He shrugged. "It's just something I know how to do."

"What's your name?" I asked the boy. "It isn't really Nobody, is it?"

"No," he said. "My name is Ronald Evans."

"That's a nice name," I said. "How old are you?"

Ronald held up one hand.

"Oh," I said. "I'm seven."

I spotted a blackberry on a nearby bush. I picked it and gobbled it up.

"My mom is in the city," I told Ronald. "And my dad is playing his trumpet on a music tour. Where are your mom and dad?"

Ronald tossed another stone into the creek. "Nowhere."

"Not that again," I said.

"They got sep-a-rated," Ronald said, hanging his head. He closed his eyes for a minute.

"That's too bad," I said. "It happened to my mom and dad, too. Last year."

Ronald looked up at me. "It did?"

"Yes," I told him. "I was sad, too."

I picked another blackberry. Ronald stood up.

"Want to help me pick berries?" I asked.

"Okay," said Ronald.

I picked a berry and dropped it into my bucket. Ronald picked one and ate it.

"No more eating," I said. "Put it in here."

I picked another berry and started singing, "Fat berry, fat berry, come into my bucket. Fat berry, fat berry..."

"What kind of song is that?" asked Ronald.

"It's the song I sing when I'm berry picking," I explained. "My dad made it up."

I sang the song again and Ronald sang, too.

"Fat berry, fat berry, come into my
bucket."

We sang louder and louder and started
to laugh. But suddenly, we got interrupted
by a loud voice.

"Ronald!"

Ronald stopped and turned around.
"Hi, Granddad."

I turned around, too. A very tall old man, who looked like Ronald, stood on the path. *He must be Mr. Evans, the hermit*, I thought. But he didn't look like a crab at all. Even his ears were regular. And I liked his curly white hair.

"Where have you been, boy?" asked Ronald's grandfather.

"Nowhere," said Ronald.

"And who is this?" the man asked, smiling at me.

Ronald dropped his head. "Nobody."

"My name is Ginger Brown," I said, trying to be polite.

The man squinted. "Are you related to the Browns over yonder?"

I nodded.

"We were picking berries, Grandpa," Ronald piped up. "We were playing."

"Well, I guess that's okay," Ronald's grandfather said. "But you were supposed to be near the house. I got worried when I couldn't find you."

He took Ronald's hand. "Let's go home for lunch now."

Ronald waved and went with his grandfather.

I looked around and felt scared. I didn't know where the path was. And I didn't see Leo anywhere.

"Excuse me," I said, running after Ronald and his grandfather. "Do you know which way I live?"

"Come with me," said Ronald's grandfather, turning around. He walked very fast. Ronald and I followed him. In no time we were on the right path. Then lickety-split we were at the edge of the woods right by Mama and Papa Brown's field.

"That was short," I said in surprise.

"Your grandfolks and I are neighbors," said Ronald's grandfather. He scowled. "A long time ago we were friends." He took Ronald's hand and pulled him away.

"Bye," I called out.

I walked through the field to the farmhouse. Leo ran out of the woods, chasing a squirrel.

Mr. Evans looked like a regular person, I thought. But I knew he was a hermit. And he was angry about something.

The Fort

The next day, Leo and I bumped into Ronald at the edge of the woods.

"Hi," I said.

"Hi."

"Leo and I were just out for a walk," I told him.

Ronald stooped down and gave Leo a pat. "Nice cat," he said.

I gave Leo a pat, too. "He's not just a cat," I told Ronald. "Leo's more like a friend. Especially since there aren't any kids to play with around here."

Ronald stood up. "*I'm* a kid."

I smiled at him and he smiled back. "So let's play," I said.

"Let's play trucks," Ronald said.

"I don't have any trucks," I told him.

"We can *be* trucks," said Ronald. "That's what me and my dad do." He ran around in circles, making truck noises. I did it, too.

After a while, I got tired of playing trucks. "Let's build a fort," I said.

"What's a fort?" asked Ronald.

"It's like a house. Come on, I'll teach you. We can build it right there." I pointed to a fallen tree trunk. There were lots of branches on it and a big space underneath.

"Help me get some sticks," I said.

We walked around picking up sticks. Then I taught Ronald how to place the sticks across the branches.

"That's the roof," I told him. "My dad taught me how to do this."

"Now what?" Ronald asked when we'd finished the roof.

"Now we go inside," I said. I crawled

beneath the branches. I reached out and pulled Leo in with me.

"Are there spiders in there?" asked Ronald.

"I don't see any spiders," I said.

Ronald crawled in and sat down beside me. The leaves on the branches looked like curtains.

Just then, a little bird hopped by and Leo jumped out.

"Don't worry. Leo only *chases* birds. He never catches them," I told Ronald.

"Isn't this cozy?" I said, settling back in the fort.

"I guess so," said Ronald.

"Look," I said, finding a funny-shaped stick. "This could be our telephone." I put the stick next to my ear. "Hello, Ronald," I said, "this is your mommy."

Ronald looked very puzzled.

"It's just pretend," I whispered.

"How are you?" I asked, trying to sound like a grownup.

Ronald giggled. "Fine."

"Guess what I'm going to do when you come back home?"

"What?"

"I'm going to take you to the circus!"

I hung up the telephone.

Ronald looked sad. "My mommy and daddy said they were coming to get me," he said. "But they didn't come yet."

"Did they call you on the telephone?" I asked.

"One time they did." Ronald sighed.

"That's okay," I said, patting his shoulder. "They're probably busy. That's what happens when parents get separated.

Don't worry. They still love you."

"They do?" said Ronald.

"My parents still love me," I said.

Then we heard Papa Brown's voice.

"Yo, Ginger! Ginger girl! Where are you?"

"That's my grandfather," I whispered. "Let's keep hiding. Then when he comes, we'll jump out."

Ronald smiled. I saw Papa Brown's big work boots through the leaves.

"Now, where could that girl be?" Papa Brown muttered.

"Boo!" I burst out of the fort.

Ronald ran out of the fort, too, and started laughing.

"So *there* you are!" said Papa Brown. He tickled me under the arms. "You scared the life out of me!"

I laughed and ran away from him.

"And who's this?" he asked, looking at Ronald.

"Nobody," Ronald said in a small voice.

"Nobody?" Papa Brown repeated.

"He's shy," I said. "His name is Ronald Evans."

"Evans?" said Papa Brown.

"His grandfather is the hermit," I whispered.

"You don't say," said Papa Brown. He walked over to Ronald and held out his hand. "Glad to meet you, Ronald."

Ronald shook Papa Brown's hand.

"We built a fort," I said.

"I see. So that's what you've been up to all morning," said Papa Brown. "You must be hungry. Come on in for a sandwich. Ronald can come, too."

"No, thanks," Ronald said.

"Oh, come on," I said. "You don't have to be shy."

"No," Ronald said. He quickly looked

at Papa Brown, then looked away.

"Let's go, Ginger," said Papa Brown. "You can play with Ronald later."

"But I want to play with him now."

"Five more minutes, then," said Papa Brown.

Papa Brown went into the house. Ronald sat down on the ground.

"Is that your *real* grandfather?" he asked.

"One of my real grandfathers," I said.

"But he's white," said Ronald.

"So what?"

He pointed to my face. "You're not white."

"I know that," I said. "But that doesn't mean he isn't my grandfather."

"I don't know any white people," said Ronald. "Only on television."

"Anybody can be a grandfather," I said. "It doesn't matter what color they are. My grandfather in the city isn't white at all. He's brown."

"Which one do you like the best?" asked Ronald. "The white one or the brown one?"

I thought for a minute. Papa Brown had taught me how to swim and swimming was really fun. But Granddaddy Gray had taught me how to read much better.

"I think I like them both the best," I said, "even though they're different. They like each other, too."

"That's nice," said Ronald.

He picked a rock up off the ground. He tossed it high in the air.

"*My* grandfather and *your* grandfather

don't like each other at all," Ronald said, running to catch his rock.

"They don't?" I said, running after him.

"My granddad said that he and your grandfather had a big fight one time," said Ronald.

"They did?"

"And ever since then," said Ronald, "they haven't been friends."

Ronald put the rock into his pocket and walked into the woods. "I'll see you tomorrow," he said.

I waved. "See you tomorrow."

I really liked Ronald. And Ronald liked me. Why didn't our grandfathers like each other?

The One That Got Away

The next morning, a loud crash woke me up. Leo and I leaped out of bed.

"Mama Brown! Mama Brown!" I called.

Mama Brown was waiting at the foot of the stairs. She hugged me. "Shh, it's only thunder. Look," she said, taking me to the window, "there's a big storm outside."

Raindrops were banging against the pane. The wind was blowing my swing up high. "I never saw a storm like this be-fore," I said.

"Storms in the country seem more fierce than storms in the city," said Mama Brown.

We went upstairs so that I could get dressed. Then we came back down. I saw lightning at the window while I was eat-ing my oatmeal.

"We'll have to find something to do on this rainy day," said Mama Brown.

"Can I play with Ronald?" I said.

"Ronald must be your new friend," said Mama Brown. "Papa Brown told me about him."

"He lives with his grandfather, Mr. Evans," I said. "But Mr. Evans isn't really a hermit. He doesn't look like a crab mon-ster."

Mama Brown chuckled. "A hermit isn't a person who looks like a crab. He's a person who likes to keep all to himself."

"But he doesn't live by himself," I said. "He lives with Ronald."

"I suppose you're right," said Mama Brown, "but for a long time Mr. Evans was alone."

"Papa Brown and Mr. Evans had a fight," I said.

"I know," said Mama Brown. "But that doesn't mean that you and Ronald can't be friends."

"But why can't Papa Brown and Mr. Evans be friends, too?" I asked.

Mama Brown shook her head. "It all started with a fish that kept getting away," she said. "Ask Papa Brown about it."

After breakfast, Mama Brown and I

went into the living room. I got my crayons and paper and pieces of art. Mama Brown held up one of my drawings.

"This is nice," she said. "Is this you and your mommy and daddy and Leo?"

"Yes," I said. "But it's not finished."

"Why don't you finish now?" Mama Brown said.

I sat at the kitchen table while Leo slept by the stove. Mama Brown sat in the rocking chair and knitted a winter cap for me. I was going to take it home when my mom came to get me.

I finished coloring Leo orange. Then I drew Nana and Granddaddy Gray, my grandparents in the city. I gave them brown skin and big smiles like my mom's. Then I drew Papa Brown in his straw hat and Mama Brown in a pair of high-heeled shoes.

"All finished," I said. I showed Mama Brown my work.

"What a wonderful picture," said Mama Brown with a laugh. "But I don't own a pair of high-heeled shoes."

"I thought I would give you some," I said.

"Well, thank you," said Mama Brown. "Let's hang this picture on the wall."

"Okay," I said.

She hung it up on the wall with some tape. I thought it looked very nice there.

Papa Brown came in out of the rain. His slicker and hat were dripping wet.

"How are the horses?" asked Mama Brown.

"Fine, now that the thunder has

stopped," Papa Brown said. "And I've fed all the animals. All but the pigs, that is."

I jumped up from the table. "Can I help you feed them?"

"Sure," said Papa Brown. "Get on your rain gear."

I put on my yellow boots and slicker and went outside. Papa Brown had a bucket of pig slops. It was only raining a little bit, but the ground was very soggy.

Papa Brown and I walked over to the pigpen. "Here you go," he said, handing me the bucket.

When the pigs saw that I had their food, they all came running. One of them slipped on the ground and got covered with mud.

I emptied the food into the trough.

The pigs all began grunting and eating as fast as they could.

"There you are," said Papa Brown. "Nice little piggies." He gave me a pat on the shoulder. "Good work, Ginger."

"Thank you," I said. I watched the pigs for a while. But I couldn't stop thinking about Papa Brown's fight with Mr. Evans. "Why don't you like Ronald's grandfather?" I asked.

"I like him," said Papa Brown. "We had a disagreement, that's all."

"About what?"

"It's a long story. Let's take a walk," said Papa Brown. He took my hand. We walked into the woods, to the creek where I had played with Ronald.

"This creek belongs to both the Browns and the Evanses," said Papa

Brown. "Our land is on this side and theirs is on the other. A great big granddaddy trout used to live here."

"What happened to it?" I asked.

"That was what the fight was all about," said Papa Brown. "For years, Evans and I had both been trying to catch that fish. But the fish kept getting away. Then one day, I caught it."

"Was it a really big fish?" I asked.

Papa Brown held his hands far apart. "This big!"

"Did you and Mama Brown eat it?" I asked.

"No," said Papa Brown. "I had to give it to Mr. Evans."

"Why?"

"The trout was on the end of *his* fishing line."

"How could that be if you caught it?" I asked.

"Mr. Evans asked me to hold his line for him while he went to get some more bait."

"And that's when the fish swam onto the hook?"

"Yes," said Papa Brown. "I felt a bite and didn't let go. I was reeling it in when Mr. Evans came back. It was the grand-daddy trout. Mr. Evans was hopping mad."

"Why?"

"He said I should have waited until he came back, so that he could bring the fish in. I guess I should have waited for him."

"And that was it? That was the fight?"

"From that day on, we stopped speaking to each other. Evans was mad because

I caught the fish," said Papa Brown. "I was mad because I had to give it away."

Papa Brown took my hand and we started back to the house. I thought the fight he'd had with Mr. Evans was silly.

Wasn't a friend worth more than a fish?

The Broken Feather

The next day the sky was sunny. I ran outside to play. When I got to the fort, Ronald was waiting.

"Hi," he said. "The storm messed up our fort."

Our stick roof was all over the place. "We can fix it," I said.

We picked up the sticks and put them back.

"Our floor is wet," said Ronald.

I peeked underneath the branches.

"Let's wait for it to dry out," I said.

Ronald climbed onto the fallen tree trunk that used to be part of our fort. He walked back and forth, holding his arms out for balance.

"Our grandfathers had a fight about a fish," I said.

"I know," said Ronald. "My granddad told me."

"Isn't that silly?" I said.

"Silly," said Ronald.

"Fighting about a fish," I said with a laugh. "That's funny."

Ronald laughed. "Yes, that's funny."

"But you and I are still friends," I said. "Right?"

"Right," said Ronald. "We wouldn't fight about a fish."

"I certainly wouldn't fight over a fish,"

I said. "Even if it belonged to me because I caught it."

"I wouldn't fight over a fish either," said Ronald. "Even if it belonged to me because it was on my fishing pole."

"Come on," I said. "Let's play Mother May I."

"I know that game," he said. "I'll be the mother."

"No, I'll be the mother."

"I could be the mother, too," Ronald said.

"I'm older than you are, Ronald," I said. "Go over there." I pointed to a spot next to a tall tree.

Ronald did what I told him to do. "Take three giant steps," I hollered.

"Mother, may I?" he shouted.

"Yes, you may," I shouted back.

Ronald took three giant steps in the mud.

"You're good at this," I said. "Now, take five umbrella twirls!"

"What's an umbrella twirl?" Ronald asked, running over.

I twirled around and around. "Like this," I said.

Ronald twirled and twirled.

"Wait!" I said. "You didn't say Mother, may I!"

"Mother, may I?" shouted Ronald, twirling some more. I had told him to do five twirls, but he had done six and he was still twirling.

"Watch out," I said. "Don't get dizzy."

"I am dizzy," he said, almost falling down.

I ran over to catch him. "Be still for a

minute," I said, holding his arm. We both stood still. We both looked down at the ground.

"Look!" said Ronald.

"Look!" I said.

We both bent down at once.

"I saw it first," I said, grabbing at a shiny black feather.

"No, you didn't," Ronald said, grabbing the feather's other end.

"Let go," I said. "This feather's good luck."

"But I found it," said Ronald.

"No, you didn't," I said, trying to take the feather away.

I pulled as hard as I could. Ronald pulled hard, too. The feather broke.

"Now look what you did," I said. I let go and my half of the feather fell to the ground.

"I didn't break it," said Ronald, with tears in his eyes.

"You were holding it too tight," I said.

"*You* were holding it, too."

"But it was mine," I argued.

Ronald stood up and put his hands on

his hips. He looked angry. "It wasn't yours because I saw it first!" he hollered.

"Well, it's in my field," I hollered back. "Anything that's in my field belongs to me! And that means feathers, too!

"Anyway," I continued, "your grand-

daddy stole my granddaddy's fish."

"That fish was *my* granddaddy's fish!" said Ronald. "And anyway, you're stupid!"

"You're stupid, too!" I said.

"You're not my friend anymore!"

Ronald pushed me onto the ground and fell on top of me. I pulled his hair and he pulled mine.

"I'm going to tell my granddad!" cried Ronald.

"Tell him! He's just an old hermit!"

"And yours has white skin!" screamed Ronald.

"So what?!" I screamed back. "You're just a Nobody Boy!"

Ronald started crying. "No, I'm not!" he said, running away. I ran away, too.

I thought Ronald was my friend. But he wasn't!

6

Friends and Neighbors

"Papa Brown! Papa Brown!" I cried. I ran into the barn. Papa Brown was brushing the horses.

"What is it, Ginger?" he said.

"Ronald is mean. I don't like him anymore."

Papa Brown put down his brush. "I thought that you and Ronald were friends. Did you two have a fight?"

"Yes," I said. "Ronald broke my

feather. On purpose." I started to cry.

"There, there," said Papa Brown. "I'm sure Ronald didn't mean to break it."

"Yes, he did," I said. "And he pulled my hair."

"I see," said Papa Brown. "Did you pull *his* hair?"

"Yes," I said. "And I'm not going to play with him anymore."

Papa Brown took his handkerchief out of his pocket. He wiped my eyes.

"I think you and Ronald should talk things over," said Papa Brown. "Let's go pay him a visit. It would be a shame to lose a friend over one argument."

Papa Brown took my hand. We walked across the field and into the woods. On the path, we bumped into Ronald and Mr. Evans.

"Hello, Evans," said Papa Brown.

"Hello, Brown," said Mr. Evans.

Ronald looked at me and then looked away.

"We were just coming to see you," said Mr. Evans.

"And we were coming to see *you*," said Papa Brown.

"Seems as if the two children have had an argument," Papa Brown said.

"Something about a feather," muttered Mr. Evans.

"It was mine," I said.

"No," said Ronald. "The feather was mine because I found it."

"No, I found it," I said.

"Hush," said Papa Brown, putting a hand on my shoulder. "Where is the feather now?"

"I don't know," I said. "Do you know where it is, Ronald?"

"No," said Ronald.

Mr. Evans rubbed his chin. "It must not be a very important feather, then."

"Certainly not important enough to lose a friend over," said Papa Brown.

Mr. Evans tapped Ronald on the shoulder. "Why don't you say that you're sorry to Ginger and shake hands."

"Sorry," said Ronald. He put out his hand.

"Your turn, Ginger," said Papa Brown.

"Sorry," I said, shaking Ronald's hand.

"That was a silly fight," I said.

"It was silly," he said.

"Anyway," I said, "there are lots of other feathers for us to find."

"And that feather broke," said Ronald.

"Now, that's the way friends should act," said Papa Brown. "Can't let a little feather come between you."

I cleared my throat. "And how about a little fish?"

Papa Brown looked at me and then he looked at Mr. Evans. "Whatever did happen to that granddaddy trout, Evans?" he asked. "Did you eat him?"

"I tried to," said Mr. Evans. "But I was so mad at you, I almost choked on it."

"You don't say?" said Papa Brown.

"Probably didn't taste like much," said Mr. Evans.

Mr. Evans chuckled. Papa Brown chuckled, too. Ronald and I just smiled.

7
Worms

"Come on," said Papa Brown. "The soil's still damp. Today's a good worm day." He was holding two fishing poles. Mama Brown gave me my cap and a shovel and a little can.

"The can is for the worms," she said, taking one of the poles out of Papa Brown's hand.

My grandparents and I walked into the woods. We walked down the path in a straight line. First Papa Brown, then Mama Brown, then me. The next thing I knew, we were at the creek.

Mr. Evans was there, too.

And so was Ronald.

"Hi, Evans," Papa Brown said. "I'm glad you could make it."

"Me too," Mr. Evans said. "Been a long time since you and I went fishing."

Mama Brown walked over to Ronald. "Hi there, Ronald!"

"Hi," Ronald said, smiling up at her.

Papa Brown held out his hand to Mr. Evans.

"It's high time we patched things up," he said. He and Mr. Evans shook hands.

"That's more like it," said Mama Brown, smiling.

"I agree," said Mr. Evans. "And we

have Ginger and Ronald to thank."

"You do?" I said.

"That was a silly fight you had. It taught us how silly *we* had been," explained Mr. Evans.

"We couldn't expect you two to shake hands if *we* wouldn't," Papa Brown added.

"So," said Mama Brown. "Let's do some fishing!"

"Yes, indeed," said Papa Brown. "But first, how about some bait?"

Ronald and I dug for worms. We found lots of them. I thought they were cute. We put them into the can with some dirt. Then Mama and Papa Brown and Mr. Evans put the worms on their fishing hooks.

"Ginger, do you want to fish?" Mr. Evans asked, offering me a fishing pole.

"No, thanks." I felt sorry for the worms.

"How about you, Ronald?" asked Papa Brown. "I bet you're a very good fisherman."

"Thanks," said Ronald. "But I don't want to fish if Ginger doesn't want to."

Ronald and I ran downstream. He picked up a flat stone and threw it. The stone skipped across the water and made three big circles.

"Your granddaddy is nice," said Ronald. "He said I was a good fisherman."

He picked up another stone and skipped it.

"I wish I could do that," I said.

"I can show you how," said Ronald.

Ronald taught me how to hold the stone. He showed me just how to throw it.

On the second try, my stone made three big circles.

"I did it!" I said.

Ronald and I skipped stones in the creek while the grownups fished upstream. I saw Mama Brown reel in a long silvery fish. Then Papa Brown caught one, and so did Mr. Evans. By the time they had finished, there were five fish lying on the ground.

"Five fish!" said Ronald, running over.

"I think I got the biggest one," said Mama Brown, holding up the long fish she had caught.

"Now we have to cook them," said Ronald.

"These fish should be good eating," said Papa Brown. "But I don't think we have enough for a fish fry, though."

"Maybe enough for a small fish fry," said Mr. Evans.

"There are five fish," I pointed out, "and *five* of us."

"I'll fry the fish if you folks will come over for supper," said Mr. Evans.

Mama Brown smiled. "We'll bring dessert."

The grownups packed up the fishing gear. Ronald and I ran downstream. There was time to skip one more rock.

Good-bye

I was in the kitchen with Mama Brown. We were getting ready to go to Ronald's. Mama Brown was taking a hot blackberry pie out of the oven. I was putting the finishing touches on a present for Ronald.

I was giving him my best picture, the one of my family.

"What are you doing?" asked Mama Brown. "I thought you were through drawing that picture. Isn't it finished?"

"Since I'm going to give it to Ronald," I said, "I had to put one more person in the picture."

I had drawn a boy with a smiling face. I drew him petting Leo. I colored the boy's hair black. I colored his shorts blue and drew stripes on his T-shirt.

"That's nice," said Mama Brown.

Papa Brown came into the kitchen. He had on a dress shirt. He sniffed the air. "At least I know that the dessert will be good. Hope Evans knows how to cook. He's been living alone for a mighty long time."

Mama Brown laughed. "I'm sure Mr. Evans will make a fine supper," she said.

And he did!

When we got to Ronald's house, everything smelled wonderful. There was a red tablecloth on the table. Ronald was pouring milk for us and Mr. Evans was at the stove, frying fish.

"Howdy, folks!" he called out. "Five fried fish, coming right up!"

Besides fish, we had corn and bread and potatoes and tomatoes. For dessert, we had Mama Brown's blackberry pie.

"Mighty fine supper," said Papa Brown, patting his stomach.

"Delicious," Mama Brown said.

"Thank you," said Mr. Evans. "Now Ronald has some news for us."

"What's your news, Ronald?" I asked.

"My mommy and daddy called me on the phone," he said.

"That's nice," I said. I knew that Ronald had wanted to talk to his parents.

"Tell them the rest of your news," said Mr. Evans. "People should share good news."

Ronald smiled again. But this time he spoke softly. "They're coming to get me in two days. And they're not separated anymore."

"What wonderful news," said Mama Brown.

I felt a little lump in my throat. Ronald was going back home right away. I was going to miss him. And not only that—his parents had stopped being separated. That's what I wanted my parents to do. I felt sad for myself.

But I still felt happy for Ronald.

"This would be a good time for you to give Ronald his present, Ginger," said Mama Brown.

I ran and grabbed my picture by the door.

"This is my best picture," I said. I gave it to Ronald. Mr. Evans came over to look at it.

"I want you to have it," I told Ronald.

"Thank you," he said.

I pointed out all the people in my family: Mommy and Daddy, me and Leo, Nana and Granddaddy Gray, and Mama and Papa Brown.

"Nice-looking family," said Mr. Evans,

"but you haven't told us who the little boy is."

"Is it your brother?" asked Ronald.

"I don't have a brother," I said.

Ronald looked at the boy in the picture. "He has a T-shirt like mine," he said. "Oh! It's *me!*"

"I know that you aren't in my family," I told him. "But if I had a brother...I'd want him to be like you."

Then Ronald smiled the biggest smile.

Two days later, Ronald went home. We promised to keep in touch. Ronald said he would ask his mother and father to help him write me a letter. I got his telephone number and told him that I would call him.

Two weeks later, Mommy came to get

me and Leo. I kissed Mama and Papa Brown good-bye. They waved as we drove away.

"Ginger, what was your favorite part of vacation?" Mommy asked.

"Playing with Nobody," I said.

"Nobody?"

I giggled. "It's a long story."

"Tell me about it," said Mommy. "It's a long drive back to the city."

So I began…

He said his name was Nobody. But he was Somebody. Ronald Evans—a boy I met down-the-country. Ronald Evans—my new friend.

About the Author

Friendship is very important to Sharon Dennis Wyeth. One of her best friends is her younger brother, Kevin. When she wrote this book, she modeled Ronald's character after him.

"He was very shy, but we had a special connection," Ms. Wyeth says. "Our friendship was a great comfort when our parents separated. I wanted Ginger to experience that kind of bond, too."

Ms. Wyeth lives with her husband, Sims, their daughter, Georgia, and their new puppy, Roscoe, in New Jersey.